Dow/oy

ase return / renew date shown.

D0229083

STAR WARS™

JOURNEY THROUGH SPACE

Written by Ryder Windham

Penguin
Random
House

Senior Editor Tori Kosara
Designer Mark Richards
Pre-production Producer Marc Staples
Senior Producer Alex Bell
Managing Editor Laura Gilbert
Managing Art Editor Maxine Pedliham
Art Director Lisa Lanzarini
Publisher Julie Ferris
Publishing Director Simon Beecroft

For Lucasfilm
Executive Editor Jonathan W. Rinzler
Art Director Troy Alders
Story Group Rayne Roberts, Pablo Hidalgo, Leland Chee

Reading Consultant
Maureen Fernandes

First published in Great Britain in 2015 by
Dorling Kindersley Limited
80 Strand, London, WC2R 0RL

10 9 8 7 6 5 4 3 2 1
001–276529–Feb/15

Page design Copyright © 2015 Dorling Kindersley Limited
A Penguin Random House Company

© and TM 2015 LUCASFILM LTD.
All rights reserved. Used under authorisation.

A CIP catalogue record for this book
is available from the British Library.

ISBN: 978-0-24118-633-6

Printed and bound in China by South China Printing Company Ltd.

www.starwars.com
www.dk.com

A WORLD OF IDEAS:
SEE ALL THERE IS TO KNOW

Contents

Planet Profiles

Come on a journey through space to the *Star Wars* galaxy. It is far, far away. There are many stars and planets in this galaxy. Each planet is different. Let's take a closer look.

TATOOINE
DESERT PLANET

Number of Suns:	2
Number of Moons:	3
Population:	200,000
Environment:	desert
Climate:	hot and dry
Famous for:	podracing

HOTH
ICE PLANET

Number of Suns:	1
Number of Moons:	3
Population:	fewer than 10
Environment:	icy
Climate:	cold and snowy
Famous for:	large glaciers

KASHYYYK

FOREST PLANET

Number of Suns:	1
Number of Moons:	3
Population:	**56 million**
Environment:	**tropical forest**
Climate:	**warm and wet**
Famous for:	**fierce warriors**

MUSTAFAR

VOLCANO PLANET

Number of Suns:	1
Number of Moons:	0
Population:	**20,000**
Environment:	**volcanic**
Climate:	**extremely hot**
Famous for:	**metal mines**

Coruscant

Coruscant is the most important planet. It is covered by one enormous city.

All the buildings in the city are gleaming skyscrapers.

Many important people live here.
Powerful Jedi Knights call this
place home.
The Jedi High Council has
important meetings in a temple
on Coruscant.

The Jedi High Council

ADI GALLIA
Adi knows many important people who can help the Council.

SAESEE TIIN
Saesee has a special skill. He sees things that have not yet happened.

YODA
Jedi Master Yoda leads the High Council. He is very powerful.

KI-ADI-MUNDI
Ki-Adi-Mundi is one of the most experienced members on the council.

MACE WINDU
Mace is wise. He joined the Council at a very young age.

YADDLE

Yaddle is a very wise Jedi Master. She is also kind and patient.

YARAEL POOF

Yarael likes to play mind tricks on the other Council members.

The Jedi High Council members meet at the Jedi Temple, which is on the planet Coruscant.
The most skilled and wise Jedi sit on the Council. There are always 12 seats. If a member dies or leaves, a new member is chosen to replace them.

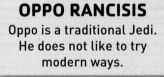

OPPO RANCISIS

Oppo is a traditional Jedi. He does not like to try modern ways.

PLO KOON

Plo has great fighting skills. He is also an amazing pilot.

EETH KOTH

Eeth is highly intelligent. He always uses his mind for good.

9

Naboo

People and Gungans live
on the planet Naboo.
The people live in beautiful
cities on the land.

The Gungans live in
underwater cities.
They can walk
on land, too,
although some
are a bit clumsy!
Jar Jar Binks
is a Gungan.

Tatooine

The planet Tatooine is
covered by a dusty desert.
Two suns shine in the sky so
it is very hot.
There is not much water on
this planet.

Tatooine is a meeting place.
Space travellers visit the planet
from all over the galaxy.
People come from near and far
to watch a high-speed sport
called podracing.

Kamino

Water flooded all the land on the planet Kamino.

So the Kaminoans built their cities on strong metal poles that stick up above the water.

Kaminoans are very tall
with long, thin necks.
They ride winged
beasts to fly and
swim around their
watery planet.

Geonosis

Geonosis is not a good
place to be captured.
Prisoners are forced to fight
huge monsters in special arenas.
The fights are dangerous.

Scary beasts are brought
from other planets
to the arenas.
The Geonosians look
like insects.
They watch the fights.

Geonosian Arena Beasts

The beasts used in the arena on Geonosis are from far away planets. Each creature is dangerous in its own way.

REEK

HOMEWORLD: Ylesia

HEIGHT: 2.24 m (7 ft 4 in)

DIET: Herbivore (plant-eater) but forced to eat meat

HABITAT: Grassland

ACKLAY

HOMEWORLD: Vendaxa
HEIGHT: 3.05 m (10 ft)
DIET: Carnivore (meat-eater)
HABITAT: Underwater, land

HOMEWORLD: Cholganna
LENGTH: 4.5 m (14 ft 9 in)
DIET: Carnivore (meat-eater)
HABITAT: Forest

NEXU

19

Kashyyyk

Kashyyyk is a world of giant
trees and shallow lakes.
It is home to the Wookiees,
including Chewbacca and Tarfful.
Wookiees are tall and have
lots of shaggy fur.
They talk in grunts and roars.

Utapau

The planet Utapau
has lots of deep holes.
The Utapauns dig
tunnels through
rocks to join
the holes.
There are other
creatures on the planet.

Creatures called Utai live in holes in the ground. Enormous lizards called varactyl wander around the rocky land.
They are good climbers.
The Utai ride the varactyl.

Mustafar

The red planet of Mustafar
is a very hot place.
It is covered in fiery volcanoes.
Hot, melted rock called lava
flows from the volcanoes.
The sky is filled with black
smoke that blocks out the sun.

Polis Massa

The space rock known as
Polis Massa has a medical centre.
This is where space travellers
can go if they are ill.
The doctors are helped by
special robots called droids.

Medical Droids

Different kinds of droids work at
the medical centre on Polis Massa.
Each robot has a special job to do.

2-1B DROID

A 2-1B droid does lots
of things. This robot
can give patients
check-ups. It speaks
with a calm voice.

DD-13 MEDICAL ASSISTANT DROID

These droids can give
humans replacement
parts, such as hands.
The new robotic piece is
called a cybernetic part.

GH-7 DROID

These droids have many skills. They are good at giving blood tests. These tests help to find out what is making a patient ill.

MIDWIFE DROID

Midwife droids are experts at delivering babies. They make sure that the babies are safe and healthy.

FX-6 DROID

It is not always easy to tell what is wrong with a patient. An FX-6 droid can help doctors figure out what the patient needs.

Yavin 4

The moon Yavin 4 is covered
in thick jungle.
The ruins of very old buildings
called temples rise above the trees.

At one time, the soldiers
who lived on Yavin 4 kept watch
for enemy starships from
the tops of the tallest temples.

Tour the Great Temple on Yavin 4

by our Special Galaxy Reporter

There are ancient temples on Yavin 4. This moon is very far away and hard to get to. Only plants and animals live here. Not many people have seen these special buildings.

The Great Temple is tucked away deep in the jungle. It takes a long time to trek through the hot, sticky forest.

The temple is huge! Its old bricks are covered in large, twisted vines. Soft green moss also grows on the walls.

Ancient warriors built the Great Temple more than 5,000 years ago.

The Great Temple

Starships inside the temple

Soldiers once lived here. The soldiers used the inside of the temple to keep their starships safe. There were also rooms where they could eat or sleep.

Today, no one uses the temple or lives there. The Great Temple is an old but amazing building to see and explore.

33

Hoth

The ice planet Hoth is very cold.
Here, the land is covered in snow
and ice.

On Hoth, people ride around
on large beasts called tauntauns.

Wampa ice creatures live
in ice caves.
They hang the animals that
they catch from the cave roof.
Once, a wampa even captured
a Jedi Knight!

Dagobah

The planet Dagobah
is covered in thick forests
and swampy land.
The air is steamy, and it rains a lot.
There are many deadly creatures
and poisonous plants.

The Jedi Master Yoda went
to hide on Dagobah.
He lived in a small tree house.

Bird's-eye View

Yoda is the only intelligent being that lives on the planet Dagobah. But there are many unique animals, plants and places to see here.

Gnarltree bridge over lagoon

Sweet water lagoon

Yoda gathers yarum seeds from this part of the forest

Yoda's house
Yoda lives alone in a small house. The house is surrounded by swampland.

Gnarltrees
These trees have large, twisty roots. Gnarltrees grow best in swamps.

Yoghurt plants

Cave

Quicksand

DRAGON SNAKE BOG

Jubba birds use mud to make nests in the trees

Dragon snake
A giant beast called a dragon snake lives here. He hides under the water, and waits for his next meal.

Cloud City

Cloud City floats in the skies
of the planet Bespin.
Visitors come to enjoy its
lively shops, restaurants
and hotels.

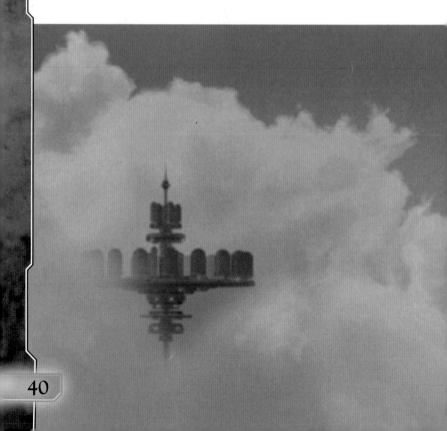

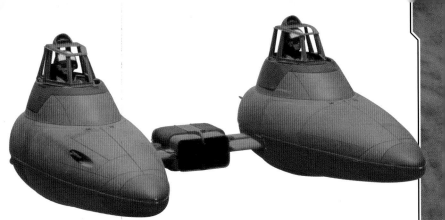

Cloud cars fly around the city.
They have room for two passengers.

Endor

The forest moon of the planet
Endor is the home of small,
furry creatures called Ewoks.
They live in the trees and
use simple tools and spears.

At night, Ewoks stay in the
villages that they build high
up in the trees.
We hope you have enjoyed your
tour of the galaxy.
Come back soon!

Glossary

Creature
An animal that is not a human being.

Desert
A dry area of land with little water and few plants.

Droid
A kind of robot.

Galaxy
A group of millions of stars and planets.

Jungle
An area of land with thick forests and lots of plants. Jungles are usually found in tropical (warm, wet) areas.

Planet
A giant ball-shaped rock that goes round a star. Naboo is a planet.

Shallow
Not very deep.

Skyscraper
A very tall building with many storeys.

Temple
A building used for religious services.

Volcano
A mountain or hill through which lava comes out.

Index

Guide for Parents

DK Reads is a three-level reading series for children, developing the habit of reading widely for both pleasure and information. These books have exciting running text interspersed with a range of reading genres to suit your child's reading ability, as required by the school curriculum. Each book is designed to develop your child's reading skills, fluency, grammar awareness and comprehension in order to build confidence and engagement when reading.

Ready for a *Beginning to Read* book
YOUR CHILD SHOULD

- be using phonics, including combinations of consonants, such as bl, gl and sm, to read unfamiliar words; and common word endings, such as plurals, ing, ed and ly.

- be using the storyline, illustrations and the grammar of a sentence to check and correct their own reading.

- be pausing briefly at commas, and for longer at full stops; and altering his/her expression to respond to question, exclamation and speech marks.

A Valuable and Shared Reading Experience

For many children, reading requires much effort but adult participation can make this both fun and easier. So here are a few tips on how to use this book with your child.

TIP 1 Check out the contents together before your child begins:

- Read the text about the book on the back cover.
- Read through and discuss the contents page together to heighten your child's interest and expectation.
- Briefly discuss any unfamiliar or difficult words on the contents page.

- Chat about the non-fiction reading features used in the book, such as headings, captions, recipes, lists or charts.

This introduction helps to put your child in control and makes the reading challenge less daunting.

TIP 2 Support your child as he/she reads the story pages:

- Give the book to your child to read and turn the pages.
- Where necessary, encourage your child to break a word into syllables, sound out each one and then flow the syllables together. Ask him/her to reread the sentence to check the meaning.
- When there's a question mark or an exclamation mark, encourage your child to vary his/her voice as he/she reads the sentence. Demonstrate how to do this if it is helpful.

TIP 3 Praise, share and chat:

- The factual pages tend to be more difficult than the story pages, and are designed to be shared with your child.
- Ask questions about the text and the meaning of the words used. Ask your child to suggest his/her own quiz questions. These help to develop comprehension skills and awareness of the language used.

A FEW ADDITIONAL TIPS

- Try and read together every day. Little and often is best. After 10 minutes, only keep going if your child wants to read on.
- Always encourage your child to have a go at reading difficult words by themselves. Praise any self-corrections, for example, "I like the way you sounded out that word and then changed the way you said it, to make sense."
- Read other books of different types to your child just for enjoyment and information.

Have you read these other great books from DK?

BEGINNING TO READ

Find out about
the amazing
creatures from the
Star Wars™ galaxy.

Meet a band of
rebels, brave
enough to take on
the Empire!

Hard hats on!
Watch the
machines build
a new school.

STARTING TO READ ALONE

Meet the heroes of
Chima™ and help
them find the
Legend Beasts.

Meet the
sharks who live
on the reef or
pass through.

Follow Chris
Croc's adventures
from a baby to
a mighty king.